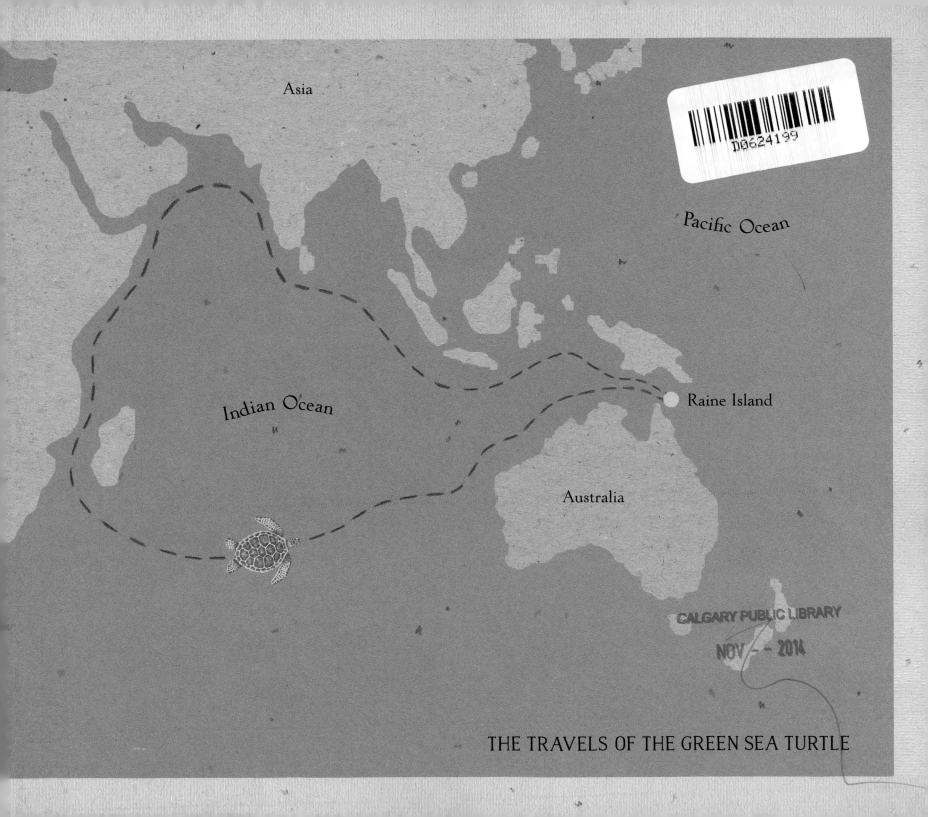

Asia

Pacific Ocean

Indian Ocean

⬤ Raine Island

Australia

THE TRAVELS OF THE GREEN SEA TURTLE

AUTHOR'S NOTE:
The Green Sea Turtle gets its name from the
green color beneath its shell or 'carapace.'

Copyright © 2014 by Gerstenberg Verlag, Hildesheim, Germany.
First published in Germany under the title *Die Grüne Meeresschildkröte*.
English translation copyright © 2014 by NorthSouth Books Inc., New York 10016.
Text, illustrations and design by Isabel Müller, Berlin, Germany.
Consultant: Margot Wilhelmi, Sulingen, Germany

Translated by David Henry Wilson.

First published in the United States, Great Britain, Canada, Australia, and
New Zealand in 2014 by NorthSouth Books Inc., an imprint of
NordSüd Verlag AG, CH-8005 Zürich, Switzerland.

Distributed in the United States by NorthSouth Books Inc., New York 10016.
Library of Congress Cataloging-in-Publication Data is available.

ISBN: 978-0-7358-4189-5
Printed in China by Leo Paper Products Ltd.,
Heshan, Guangdong, May 2014.
1 3 5 7 9 • 10 8 6 4 2

www.northsouth.com

MIX
Papier aus verantwor-
tungsvollen Quellen
FSC® C020056

THE GREEN SEA TURTLE

Isabel Müller

North
South

IT'S NIGHT ON RAINE ISLAND, a remote location off the coast of Australia. All is quiet except for the gentle sighing of the waves. Suddenly, something moves on the shore.

Under cover of darkness, a little green turtle climbs out of her sandy cradle. She frees herself from her egg, which is about the size of a Ping-Pong ball, and digs her way up to the surface.

Ghost Crab

The little turtle's brothers and sisters have also hatched.
They must get to the water as quickly as possible, because
terrible dangers await them on the shore. The little hatchlings,
which are no more than 2 inches long, are easy prey for such
predators as the ghost crab. Instinctively the turtles hurry
toward the open sea. They are guided by the brightness of
the shining water.

Silver Gull

Phew, she made it! At last the little turtle has reached the water. But even here she is far from safe, because there are lots of sea creatures that would be only too pleased to have her for their dinner. And so in order to get to a safe refuge, she swims farther and farther out to sea. Her brothers and sisters all go their own way, because turtles are not social animals.

Redtoothed Triggerfish

Scalloped Hammerhead Shark

Sand Tiger Shark

Candy Cane Coral

Laced Moray

Common Reef Octopus

Finger Coral

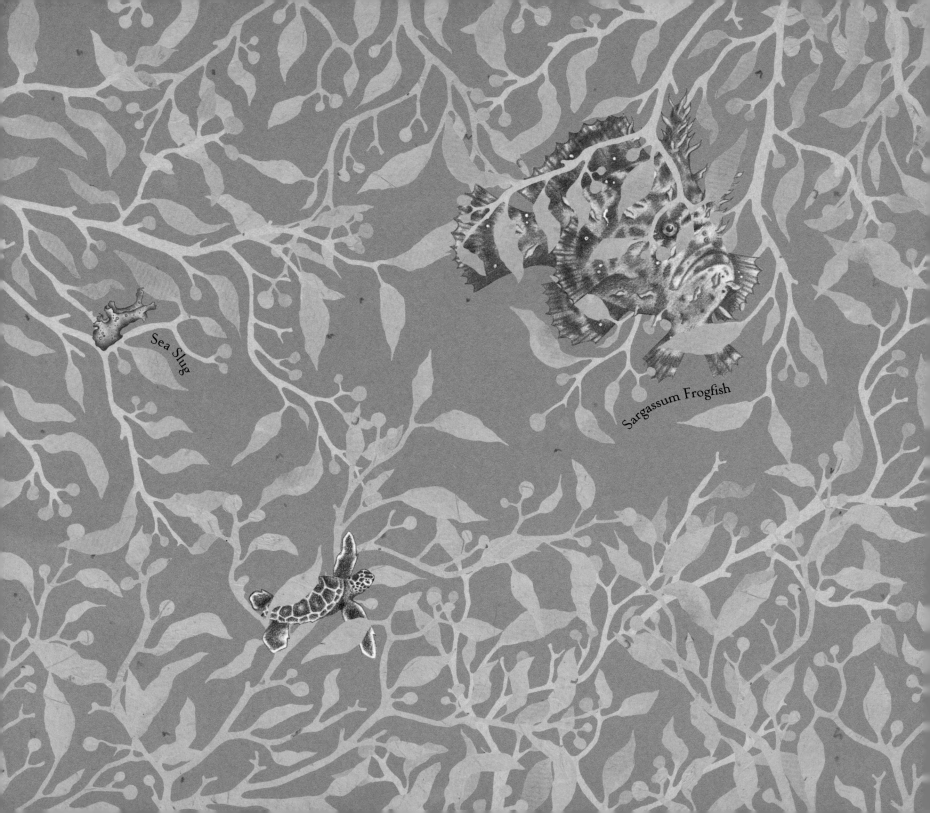

Sea Slug

Sargassum Frogfish

Double-Ended Pipefish

After swimming for many hours, the little turtle finds
a raft of drifting seaweed. This hiding place will protect her
from predators such as sharks and morays, so at last she can
rest. There are other creatures that also seek refuge in the
seaweed. That means she can find plenty of food here, such
as tiny crabs. The open sea will now be the turtle's home for
a long time.

Planehead Filefish

Swimming Crab

Our turtle has been traveling for many years, and she can now move swiftly and elegantly through the water. Her hind legs steer her, like the rudder of a boat, and her powerful front legs help her to swim very fast. She has also grown a thick shell, or carapace, so that even a large shark would crack its teeth trying to bite her.

Moon Jellyfish

Now she can venture close to the shore, even without the protection of the seaweed. Here she meets many other sea creatures, such as the mimic octopus, which sometimes defends itself against its enemies by taking on the forms of venomous animals.

Mimic Octopus

Zebra Sole

Devil Firefish

Banded Sea Krait

Pineapple Sea Cucumber

The turtle feeds only on plants now. Her favorite food is seagrass, which grows in vast underwater meadows. She shares this love of seagrass with dugongs.

Dugong

Banded Pipefish

Sea horses also live here.
They use their tails to cling to
the grass, like little monkeys.

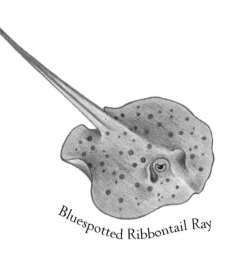

Bluespotted Ribbontail Ray

Harlequin
Filefish

On her journey from one seagrass meadow to another, the turtle swims through a coral reef. This reef is swarming with lots of brightly shining fish.

Clown Triggerfish

Whitemargin Unicornfish

Acropora Coral

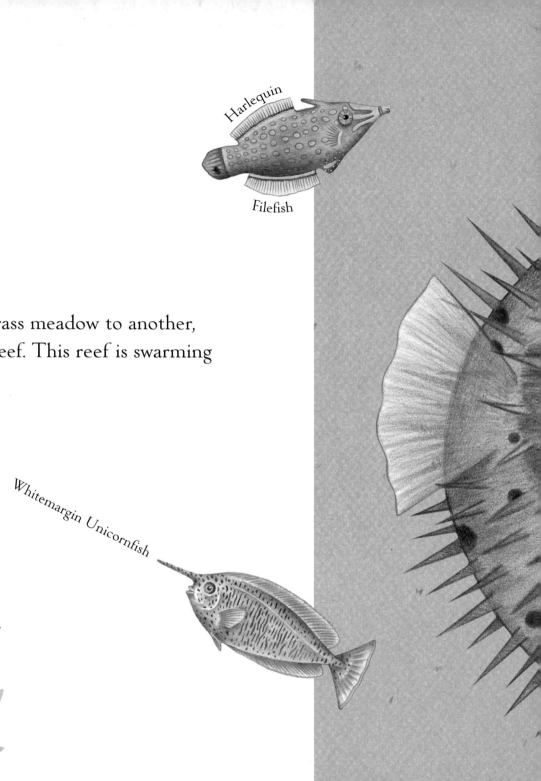

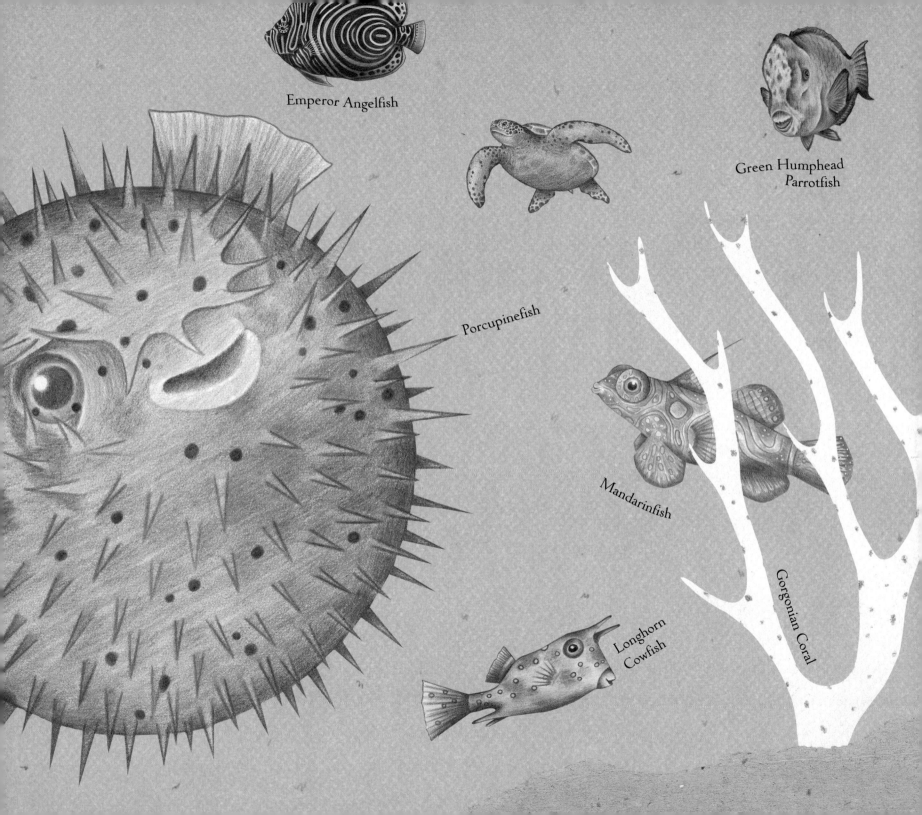

Emperor Angelfish

Green Humphead
Parrotfish

Porcupinefish

Mandarinfish

Longhorn
Cowfish

Gorgonian Coral

For twenty years our green turtle has been journeying far and wide across the ocean. Suddenly, early one summer, she feels the need to return to the shore on which she was born. During all these years, however, she has traveled so far that there are now thousands of miles between her and Raine Island. Nevertheless, guided by her inner compass, she starts the long journey home.

Pyjama Slug

Fire Coral

Gorgonian Coral

Silurian Coral

Mushroom Coral

Orange Cup Coral

Humpback Whale

On the way she meets other travelers, such as the giant humpback whale. He is heading for the South Pole, where he intends to spend the summer.

Peacock Flounder

Shortly before she reaches her destination, for the first time in her life our turtle meets an adult male turtle. He was also born on Raine Island, and has had to make a journey just as long as hers. The two of them mate, and then once again they go their separate ways.

Seven to ten weeks later, and many long years after she left her birthplace, the green turtle finally returns to the shores of Raine Island. She now weighs almost 220 pounds. Again under cover of darkness, and no longer borne up by the water, she slowly and laboriously drags herself over the sand. With her hind legs she digs a deep hole. Inside the hole she lays about a hundred eggs, then shovels the sand back over them. Then she returns to the sea, leaving the eggs to the warmth of the sun and the protection of the sand. In about six weeks, the baby turtles will hatch.

Then, once more, the shores of Raine Island will witness
the start of another long journey....

The red-eared terrapin lives in the freshwater lakes of North America.

Sea turtles come from the same family as tortoises and freshwater turtles. Their bodies are perfectly adapted to life in the water, with their front and hind legs having evolved into large paddles. Over time their carapace has become flatter, so that they have lost the ability to withdraw their heads and legs into the shell.

The leopard tortoise lives in the African savannah.

There are seven kinds of sea turtle, which can be found in all tropical and subtropical oceans. All seven kinds of sea turtles travel long distances, and always return to the shore where they were born, in order to mate and lay their eggs. The sex of the baby turtles depends on the temperature of the sand in which the eggs have been laid. At above 85 degrees Fahrenheit they will be female, and if the sand is cooler, they will be male. Apart from such vegetarian foods as seagrass, most turtles also feed on small creatures like crabs and jellyfish. They must come to the surface of the water in order to breathe, but can stay underwater for several hours at a time. Turtles can live for up to a hundred years.

THE GREEN SEA TURTLE owes its name to its special feeding
habits, because the adult eats only plants. Because its flesh has been
used for centuries to make turtle soup, it is also known in some places
as the soup turtle. It can grow to a length of five feet.

THE LEATHERBACK TURTLE is the largest of all the sea turtles,
measuring up to eight feet in length and weighing up to 1,100 pounds.
It sometimes swims as far afield as the North Atlantic, and that makes
it the most widely traveled reptile in the world. Unlike the hard
carapace of its relatives, its shell is covered with a soft, leathery skin.

THE OLIVE RIDLEY SEA TURTLE and the
ATLANTIC RIDLEY SEA TURTLE are the
smallest varieties, measuring just 27 inches
in length.

THE ATLANTIC RIDLEY is very similar to
the olive Ridley, but it is only to be found on the
Atlantic coast of Mexico.

THE FLATBACK SEA TURTLE lays the largest
eggs, and its main breeding grounds are on the
northern coast of Australia.

THE HAWKSBILL SEA TURTLE is famous for the
beautiful pattern of its carapace. Its upper jaw looks like
the beak of a bird of prey.

Yum! Yum! A jellyfish! When a turtle mistakes a plastic bag for a ready-made meal, it can suffer a painful death by suffocation.

THE LOGGERHEAD SEA TURTLE has a massive head and powerful jaws with which it can easily crack open such prey as crabs and sea urchins.

Sea turtles are an endangered species. For centuries they have been hunted by humans because their meat and eggs are regarded as delicacies, and their carapaces are used to make such objects as tortoiseshell combs and eyeglass frames.

Today, all trading of these products is banned, but in some countries it continues illegally. Pollution of the sea and the development of their breeding grounds for tourism are further threats to the survival of the sea turtle, as is deep-sea fishing, because the turtles are often caught up accidentally in the fishing nets.

The tortoiseshell from loggerhead turtles was especially popular during the eighteenth and nineteenth centuries in the manufacture of everyday objects as well as ornaments.

Sea turtles have roamed the Earth for more than two hundred million years. They were even around at the same time as the dinosaurs. The largest turtle ever discovered was the Archelon. It was three times the size of a fully-grown green sea turtle.

Ammonite

Archelon

Sponge

Pteranodon

Platecarpus

Coelacanth

Sponge

Elasmosaurus

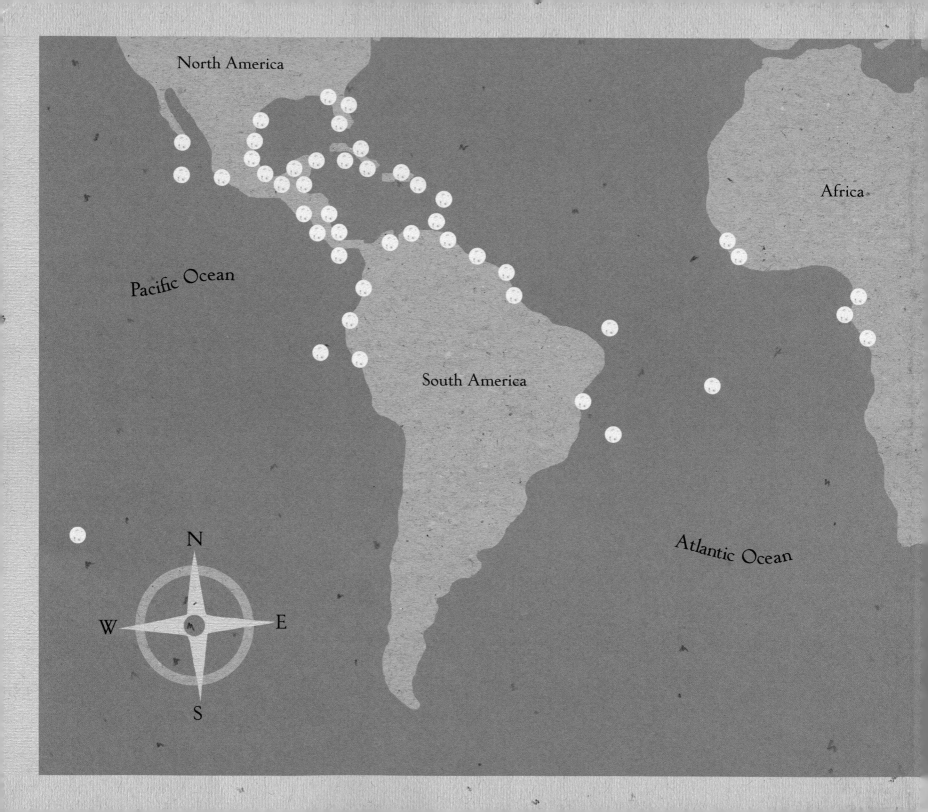

North America

Africa

Pacific Ocean

South America

Atlantic Ocean

N

W   E

S